Princess Mirror-Belle

and the Magic Shoes

Books by Julia Donaldson

The Princess Mirror-Belle series (illustrated by Lydia Monks)

Princess Mirror-Belle
Princess Mirror-Belle and the Party Hoppers
Princess Mirror-Belle and the Magic Shoes
Princess Mirror-Belle and Prince Precious Paws
Princess Mirror-Belle and the Flying Horse
Princess Mirror-Belle and the Sea Monster's Cave

Poetry

Crazy Mayonnaisy Mum
Wriggle and Roar
Shuffle and Squelch
Poems to Perform (anthology)

Plays

Play Time
Plays to Read (a series for schools)

Picture books with Lydia Monks

Sharing a Shell
The Princess and the Wizard
What the Ladybird Heard
The Rhyming Rabbit
The Singing Mermaid
Sugarlump and the Unicorn
Princess Mirror-Belle and the Dragon Pox
What the Ladybird Heard Next

JULIA DONALDSON

Princess Mirror-Belle

and the Magic Shoes

Illustrated by
LYDIA MONKS

MACMILLAN CHILDREN'S BOOKS

These stories first published 2005 in *Princess Mirror-Belle and the Magic Shoes* by Macmillan Children's Books

This edition published 2017 by Macmillan Children's Books
an imprint of Pan Macmillan
20 New Wharf Road, London N1 9RR
Associated companies throughout the world
www.panmacmillan.com

ISBN 978-1-5098-8024-9

1 3 5 7 9 8 6 4 2

A CIP catalogue record for this book is available from
the British Library.

Printed and bound by CPI Group (UK) Ltd, Croydon CR0 4YY

For Alyssa and Brooke

Contents

Chapter One

The Magic Shoes

"Hey, you! Yes, you! Turn around, look over your shoulder," sang Ellen's brother, Luke, into the microphone.

Ellen was sitting in the village hall watching Luke's band, Breakneck, rehearse for the Battle of the Bands. The hall was nearly empty, but that evening it would be packed with fans of the six different bands who were entering the competition.

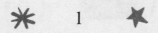

As well as being Breakneck's singer, Luke wrote most of their songs, including this one.

"It's me! Yes, me! Turn around, I'm still here," he sang. Then he wandered moodily around the stage, while the lead guitarist, Steph, played a twangy solo.

Steph, who never smiled, wore frayed baggy black trousers with a pointless chain hanging out of the pocket and a black T-shirt with orange flames on it. The solo went on and on.

"Steph's so good at the guitar," Ellen whispered to Steph's sister Seraphina, who was sitting next to her.

"I know," said Seraphina. She was two years older than Ellen and dressed very much like her brother, except that her

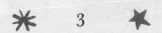

3

T-shirt had a silver skull on it. "But I bet they don't win. I don't think they should have chosen this song. It's not going to get people dancing. Steph wrote a much better one called 'Savage'."

Ellen couldn't imagine Steph writing anything dancy, but she was quite shy of Seraphina and didn't say so. Besides, she had just remembered something.

"Dancing – help! I'm going to be late for ballet!" She picked up a bag from the floor.

"You've got the wrong bag – that's mine," said Seraphina, who also went to ballet, but to a later class.

"Sorry." Ellen grabbed her own bag and hurried to the door.

At least she didn't have far to go. The ballet classes were held in a room called the studio, which was above the hall. Ellen ran up the stairs.

The changing room was empty. The other girls must be in the studio already, but Ellen couldn't hear any music so the class couldn't have started yet.

Hurriedly, she put on her leotard and ballet shoes and scooped her hair into the hairnet that Madame Jolie, the ballet teacher, insisted they all wear. Madame Jolie was very fussy about how they looked and could pounce on a girl for the smallest thing, such as crossing the ribbons on her ballet shoes in the wrong way.

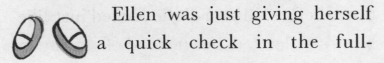

Ellen was just giving herself a quick check in the full-length mirror when a voice said, "What's happened to your feet?"

It was a voice that she knew very well. It was coming from the mirror and it belonged to Princess Mirror-Belle.

Ellen and Mirror-Belle had met several times before. Mirror-Belle looked just like Ellen's reflection, but instead of staying in the mirror as reflections usually do, she had a habit of coming out of it. She was much cheekier and naughtier than Ellen and she was always boasting about her life in the palace and the magic things that she said happened to her.

Ellen hadn't seen Mirror-Belle for a while, and she wasn't sure how pleased she was to see her now. All too often Mirror-Belle had got them both into trouble and then escaped into a mirror, leaving Ellen to take the blame.

"Mirror-Belle! You can't come to my dancing class," she said now, then added, "What do you mean about my feet anyway? What's wrong with them?"

"They're not dancing!" said Princess Mirror-Belle, leaping out of the mirror into the changing room. She was wearing an identical leotard and ballet shoes to Ellen's, and a hairnet too, though she pulled this off and flung it to the ground with a shudder, saying, "I must have walked through a spider's web." Then she began to prance around the room, pointing her toes and waving her arms.

"Stop! You'll tire yourself out before the class has even started," said Ellen.

"I can't stop. And I'm surprised that you can. I think you should take your shoes back to the elves and complain."

"What elves?" asked Ellen.

But already Mirror-Belle had opened the door to the studio and was dancing in. Ellen followed her with a sinking feeling.

The other girls in the class were standing in a line, waiting to curtsy to Madame Jolie. Ellen and Mirror-Belle joined the line. Some of the girls tittered as Mirror-Belle continued to dance up and down on the spot.

"Who's she?" asked one.

"She looks just like you, Ellen," said another.

Madame Jolie had been talking to the lady who played the piano, but now she turned round to face the class.

"*Bonjour, mes élèves*," she said.

This meant "Good day, my pupils," in French. Madame Jolie was French and she always started the class like this.

"*Bonjour, Madame*," chanted Ellen and the other girls as they dropped a curtsy to the teacher – all except Mirror-Belle, who twirled around with her arms above her head.

"Leetle girl on ze left – zat ees not a curtsy," said Madame Jolie.

"Ah, you noticed – well done." Mirror-Belle jiggled about as she spoke. "No,

I *never* curtsy – except very occasionally to my parents, the King and Queen. And I'm surprised that all these girls are curtsying to you instead of to me – or are you a princess too?"

"Zees ees not ze comedy class," replied Madame. Then her frown deepened.

"Where ees your 'airnet?" she asked.

"A *hairnet*, did you say? Why on earth should I wear one of those? The only thing I ever put on my head is a crown. I didn't wear one today, though, because . . ." Mirror-Belle paused for a second and then went on, "because one of the diamonds fell out of it yesterday and it had to go to the palace jeweller to be repaired."

Ellen wondered if this was true. She had never seen Mirror-Belle with a crown on and sometimes doubted if she really *was* a princess.

"If you forget ze 'airnet one more time you will leave ze class," warned Madame. Then she ordered the girls to go to the barre.

"We will practise ze *pliés*. First position, everyone."

Ellen and the others held the barre with their right hands and, with their heels together, turned their toes out. Then, as the piano started up, they all bent their knees and straightened up again. Ellen couldn't see Mirror-Belle, who was behind her, but she could hear a thumping sound and some stifled giggles.

"*Non, non, non!*" exclaimed Madame. She clapped her hands to stop the music and then wagged her finger at Mirror-Belle. "Why ees it zat you are jumping? I said plié, not sauté. A plié is a bend. A sauté is a jump." She demonstrated the two movements gracefully.

"It's no use telling me that," said Mirror-Belle, leaving the barre and dancing up to Madame. "It's my ballet shoes you should be talking to."

Some of the girls giggled, but Madame was not impressed. "Do not argue, and keep still!" she ordered Mirror-Belle.

"But I can't!" Mirror-Belle complained. "I did think that *you* might understand about my shoes, even if Ellen doesn't. I can see I'll have to explain."

"Zere is no need for zat," said Madame, but Mirror-Belle ignored her. Skipping around in time to her own words, she said, "They're magic shoes. As soon as I put them on, my feet start dancing and I can't stop till the soles are worn out." She twirled around and then added, "Sometimes I dance all night."

"Then why aren't they worn out already?" asked one of the girls, and received a glare from Madame.

"This is a new pair," said Mirror-Belle. "Some elves crept into the palace and made them for me in the night. I hid behind a curtain and watched them. Luckily they didn't see me. If they found

out I knew about them, they'd probably never come back. They're very shy, you see." She leaped in the air and landed with a thump. "This pair is very well made. They'll probably take ages to wear out."

Madame had had enough. "In zat case, you can go and wear zem out somewhere else," she said angrily.

"What a good idea," said Mirror-Belle. "So you're not just a pretty pair of feet after all," and she flitted and twirled her way to the door.

"Come on, Ellen!" she called over her shoulder as she danced out of the room.

Ellen hesitated. Part of her wanted to follow Mirror-Belle, to try to stop her causing too much chaos elsewhere. On the other hand, she never was very good

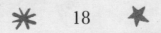

at that; usually she just got drawn into whatever trouble Mirror-Belle created. She decided to stay where she was. With a bit of luck, Mirror-Belle might get bored and go back through the changing-room mirror into her own world.

"What an *enfant terrible*!" muttered Madame. "And no 'airnet!" she added, as if this was the worst crime of all. Then she turned back to the class. "Now, *mes élèves*, we will do ze *pliés* in second position."

Ellen's mother, Mrs Page, was teaching the piano to Robert Rumbold when the doorbell rang.

"Excuse me, Robert," she said, interrupting a piece called "Boogie Woogie Bedbug", which Robert was playing very woodenly. She went to the door.

"Ellen, you're back very early – and why are you still in your dancing things?"

"I'm not Ellen, I'm Princess Mirror-Belle," said the girl on the doorstep. She danced past Ellen's mother and into the sitting room.

"Don't be silly, Ellen. And come out of there. You know you're not allowed in the sitting room when I'm teaching."

Ellen's mother had never met Mirror-Belle before. Although Ellen was always talking about her, her mother thought she was just an imaginary friend.

Robert was still playing "Boogie Woogie Bedbug", and the girl who Mrs Page thought was Ellen was slinking around the room, waggling her hips and clicking her fingers in time to the music.

"You heard me, Ellen. Go to your room and get changed. Where are your clothes anyway?"

"That's a tricky question. It depends on whether my maid is having a lazy day or not. If she is, then my clothes are still on the palace floor where I left them. If she's not, then they're hanging up in the royal wardrobe," said the girl, jumping on to the sofa and off again.

"I suppose you've left them at ballet," said Mrs Page with a sigh. "You'd better go back there now and get changed."

"That's really no way to talk to a princess, but since you're my friend's mother I'll excuse you." She danced out of the room and Ellen's mother heard the front door slam.

"I'm so sorry about that, Robert," she said.

Robert just grunted and went on playing "Boogie Woogie Bedbug". Strangely enough, the piece was now sounding much livelier than before, as if the bedbug had learned to jump at last.

"That's coming on so much better," Mrs

Page told him as she saw him out a few minutes later. "Keep practising it, and then next week you can start on 'Hip Hop Hippo'."

Just then she spotted Ellen coming round the corner towards the house. She was wearing her outdoor clothes.

"Hello, Ellen – that was very quick! You're back just in time to apologize to Robert."

"What for?" asked Ellen, looking puzzled.

"For barging in to his lesson like that."

"Oh no, don't say Mirror-Belle's been here," groaned Ellen. "Where is she now?"

"She's in your imagination – just the same as usual – so stop blaming her for everything you do wrong. In fact, if you mention Mirror-Belle one more time I won't let you go to the Battle of the Bands."

That evening Ellen, who had succeeded in not mentioning Mirror-Belle (though she kept thinking about her), was standing near the front of the village hall waiting for the second half of the Battle of the Bands to start. Three of the bands had played already, and the last of these, Hellhole, had received wild applause.

Breakneck would have to play really well to beat them.

"Do you want a Coke?" came a voice. It was Seraphina, who had pushed her way through the crowds of people to join Ellen.

"Thanks. I like your T-shirt – it's cool," said Ellen.

Seraphina was no longer wearing her skull T-shirt. This one had a green-winged snake on it.

"Did you hear what happened to my other one?" asked Seraphina. "It was stolen from the changing room while I was at my ballet class. So were my jeans. Who do you think could have taken them?"

"I've no idea," said Ellen untruthfully.

In fact, she had a very strong suspicion. Mirror-Belle must have danced back to the hall while the older girls were having their lesson and changed into Seraphina's black jeans and silver-skull T-shirt. But where was she now?

Just then the lights in the hall were dimmed and some bright-coloured ones came on over the stage.

"Hi there, pop-pickers! Welcome back to the battlefield!" said the compère, Mr Wilks, who was a geography teacher in Luke's school.

Seraphina sniggered. "He's not exactly cool, is he?" she whispered.

Ellen decided she didn't like the superior

way in which Seraphina always spoke. Mirror-Belle put on airs too, but at least she could be good fun. Ellen wondered again where she had got to.

"Put your paws together for Breakneck!" said Mr Wilks, and Ellen clapped much louder than anyone else as Luke, Steph and the other members of Breakneck slouched on to the stage.

Luke tripped up on his way to his place and everyone laughed. Ignoring them, he hunched over the microphone.

"Hey, you! Yes, you!" he began.

He was pointing at the audience, and Ellen thought he looked quite good, but she could hear him only very faintly.

Then he stopped altogether and signalled to Steph and the others to stop playing. What had gone wrong?

The sound technician came on to the stage, sighed and plugged the lead from Luke's microphone into the amplifier.

"It must have come unplugged when he tripped," said Seraphina.

Not looking too put out, Luke started again.

"Hey, you! Yes, you!

"Turn around, look over your shoulder," he sang.

A loud screeching sound accompanied his voice.

"Feedback," whispered Seraphina knowledgeably.

This time, Luke didn't stop. The sound technician fiddled about with a knob and soon Luke's voice sounded normal. In fact, he was singing really well, Ellen thought, though she probably wouldn't admit it to him afterwards. But it had not been a good beginning. Some of the audience were still laughing, and a couple of Hellhole fans tried to start up a chant of, "Get them off!"

Breakneck didn't let any of this upset them. They carried on, and by the time Steph's twangy guitar solo started quite a few people were tapping their feet and swaying. The coloured lights were flashing and some smoke started to rise from the foot of the stage.

"That's the smoke machine," said Seraphina. "It was Steph's idea."

The guitar solo came to an end at last and Luke started the "Hey, you!" chorus again.

Ellen was aware of a disturbance somewhere behind her.

"Watch out!"

"Stop pushing!"

"That was my toe!"

She turned around and saw who was

creating the fuss and bother. It was a girl dressed in black, dancing her way through the crowds. Because she was flinging her arms around, people were making way for her and soon she was at the very front of the hall.

"Turn around," sang Luke, and the girl turned around, her loose hair flying about.

"Look over your shoulder," he sang, and she stuck her chin out over her right shoulder, at the same time stamping her right foot and raising her left hand. Her wild hair was almost covering her face, but Ellen had no doubt who it was.

"Mirror-Belle, how could you?" she muttered under her breath. Just when Breakneck were beginning to impress people . . . This would ruin their chances!

But, to her surprise, a couple of girls in the front row started copying Mirror-Belle's movements, turning around whenever she did, looking over their shoulders with the same stamp and hand gesture, and pointing whenever Luke sang "Hey, you!" Some people stared at them, but others began to join in.

The dance was infectious. Very soon nearly everyone in front of Ellen seemed to be doing it. They were joining in the words of the song as well. She turned round and saw that the people behind her were dancing and singing too.

On the stage, Luke was grinning. He caught Steph's eye and mouthed something to him. Ellen knew that they were at the end of the song, but they weren't slowing down like they usually did.

"They've gone back to the beginning! They're going to sing it all over again!" she whispered to Seraphina happily.

She expected Seraphina to look happy too, but instead she was staring accusingly at Mirror-Belle.

"Have you seen what I have?" she asked. "She's wearing my clothes! She's the thief!"

She strode forward, pushing through the dancers in front of her and reaching out for the skull T-shirt, which looked more like a dress on Mirror-Belle. Just when Seraphina tried to grab it,

Mirror-Belle did another of her spins and, for the first time, noticed Ellen behind her.

"Oh, hello, Ellen. Why didn't you come with me? I've been visiting your local library. It hasn't got nearly so many books as the palace library, but that's quite good in a way, because it meant there was lots of room for dancing about. I must say, though, some of the servants in there are awfully rude."

So that's where Mirror-Belle had been! Now Ellen would dread going to the library, knowing that the librarians would think she was the naughty dancing girl they had told off.

Meanwhile, the rest of the audience were so carried away with the song and

dance that they didn't
spot that Mirror-Belle
had stopped doing the
actions along with
them. They took no
more notice of her –
apart from Seraphina,
that is, who was
making another grab
at the T-shirt.

Mirror-Belle was
too quick for her.
"Excuse me," she said, "my shoes are
taking off again!" and the next moment
she was dancing her way back through the
crowds.

Seraphina followed her, and Ellen
followed Seraphina. The rest of the

audience just went on dancing in time to the music – almost as if they were all wearing magic shoes themselves.

"Where's she gone?" asked Seraphina.

They were out of the hall now and Mirror-Belle was nowhere to be seen.

"Let's look outside," suggested Ellen.

In fact, she was pretty sure that Mirror-Belle would be on her way to the nearest mirror, the one in the changing room upstairs, but she wanted to give her a little time to escape from Seraphina. She felt a bit guilty about this – after all, Mirror-Belle had taken Seraphina's clothes – but she couldn't help being on Mirror-Belle's side.

They peered out of the front door and up and down the street.

"No," said Seraphina. "Anyway, she wouldn't go outside – she was wearing ballet shoes."

You don't know Mirror-Belle, thought Ellen, but said nothing.

"Let's look upstairs," said Seraphina,

and she led the way.

"Look! There are my clothes on the floor!" she cried, as they entered the changing room. She picked them up. "They're drenched in sweat!" she said in disgust. "You'd think she'd been dancing ever since she put them on. Here, you hold them, Ellen – I'm going to find her."

Seraphina strode into the studio, but emerged a few moments later, looking puzzled. "That's funny," she said. "She's not in there, and there's no other way out." Then, "Why are you smiling?" she asked Ellen, who was glancing at the mirror.

Ellen didn't want to tell Seraphina that she knew where Mirror-Belle had gone. She would have to explain her smile some other way.

"I'm smiling," she said, "because I'm sure Breakneck are going to win the Battle of the Bands."

Then she turned back to the mirror and quietly, so that Seraphina wouldn't hear, she whispered, "Thanks, Mirror-Belle."

Chapter Two

The Golden Goose

"Ooh, look, here comes Dad! Now he's off again – that was quick!" Ellen's granny sounded very excited. She was peering out of the window of the spare bedroom through a pair of binoculars. "He'll be back again in no time, you wait and see . . . Yes, here he is! Good old Dad!"

Granny wasn't

talking about Ellen's father, who was away in Paris with her mother, but about a blue tit that was flying in and out of a nesting box in the garden, feeding his young family.

"Here, you have a look, Ellen!"

Granny passed over the binoculars and Ellen trained them on the nesting box, which was hanging from a tree. Sure enough, she saw the little bird fly in through the hole in the box and then out again.

"Keep watching! I'll go and make the tea," said Granny.

Ellen watched the blue tit come and go

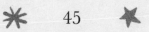

a few times, then lost interest and started experimenting with the binoculars. She found that if she looked through them the other way round, the tree with the nesting box appeared very small and far away. Everything did. She turned slowly round the bedroom, looking through the binoculars at the tiny bed, chest of drawers and wardrobe. It looked like a bedroom in a doll's house.

"And I'm the doll," she said, peering at her own shrunken reflection in the wardrobe mirror.

"Don't you mean the elephant?" came an answering voice, and out of the mirror jumped a tiny girl with a tiny pair of binoculars of her own. Although she was so small, Ellen recognized her immediately.

It was Princess Mirror-Belle.

"Mirror-Belle! You've shrunk!" Removing the binoculars from her eyes, Ellen squatted down to talk to Princess Mirror-Belle, who had climbed on to her shoe.

"Don't be silly – it's you who've grown," replied Mirror-Belle, adding, "I must say, I'm surprised to find you here at all. What are you doing at the top of a beanstalk?"

"I'm not at the top of a beanstalk," said Ellen. She was about to tell Mirror-Belle that she was at her grandparents' house, staying there for the Easter weekend, when a gruff voice called out, "Ellen! It's teatime!"

"It's the giant!" cried Mirror-Belle, clutching Ellen's ankle in alarm.

"No, it's not – it's Grandpa," said Ellen.

Mirror-Belle took no notice. "You'll have to hide me, Ellen!" she said.

"Oh, all right," said Ellen. "How about in here?" She picked Mirror-Belle up carefully and popped her into the drawer of the bedside table.

"It's much too hard," complained Mirror-Belle. "Not at all suitable for a princess. Can't you line it with velvet, or moss, or something?"

Ellen looked around. There was a box of tissues on the table. She pulled out a few. "Will these do?" she asked as she set them down in the drawer. Mirror-Belle looked doubtful, but when Grandpa's voice came again – "Ellen! Hurry up!" – she lay down on the tissues.

"Don't forget *my* tea, will you?" she said, as Ellen went out of the room. "Beanstalk-climbing is hungry work."

There were home-made scones for tea. Ellen wanted to sneak one into her pocket for Mirror-Belle, but it was difficult to find the right moment. Granny and Grandpa never seemed to take their attention off her: they kept talking to her about their two favourite subjects – the garden and the birds who visited it.

"Over four hundred daffodils we had this year," said Granny. And, "Wait till you see my new bird bath, Ellen," boasted Grandpa.

It was only when Granny called out, "Look! There they are, the rascals!" that both their heads turned to the window to look at a pair of magpies, and Ellen whisked the scone off her plate and into her pocket.

It was a while before she could give it to Mirror-Belle, since Grandpa insisted on taking her on a tour of the garden first, pointing out with pride the bird bath and the gnomes, which he had carved himself. When Ellen eventually managed to escape to her bedroom, she found Princess Mirror-Belle in a grumpy mood.

"Not very appetizing," she said, giving the scone a disapproving look.

"It's delicious," said Ellen, and broke it into crumbs.

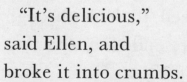

Mirror-Belle seized a handful of crumbs and stuffed them into her mouth. "The palace pastry-cook would get the sack if

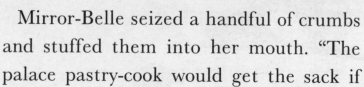 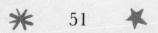

he produced anything as plain as this," she grumbled, but she ate all the crumbs swiftly and they seemed to improve her mood. "Now," she said, "it's time to look for the golden goose."

"What golden goose?" asked Ellen.

"The one that lays the golden eggs, of course. A giant stole it from the palace and I've come to get it back. I wonder where he's hidden it." Mirror-Belle picked up her tiny binoculars and put them to her eyes the wrong way round.

"You need to look through the other end for spotting birds," said Ellen.

Mirror-Belle looked put out for a second, but then retorted, "I certainly do not. Everything here is terrifyingly huge already. If I made it look any bigger I'd probably die of fright. This is giant land, remember."

Ellen laughed. "Do you think *I'm* a giant then?" she asked.

"That's been puzzling me," said Mirror-Belle. "No. I think that the giants must have been fattening you up to eat you. But don't worry, I know how to make a special shrinking potion. Could you get hold of some petrol and shoe polish, and a few spoonfuls of marmalade?"

"*No*," said Ellen. "It would

just get me into trouble, like that time in the bathroom."

She was remembering the very first time they had met. Mirror-Belle had appeared out of the bathroom mirror and persuaded Ellen to mix up all sorts of things in the bath.

Mirror-Belle looked slightly disappointed but then said, "While we're on the subject of baths, it's about time that I had mine." She yawned, and added, "And then bed, I think. We can always hunt for the golden goose tomorrow."

So Mirror-Belle was planning to stay the night! Ellen wasn't sure how she felt about that. Still, a bath couldn't do any harm. Ellen pointed to the washbasin in the corner of the bedroom. "Will you have your bath in there?" she asked.

"Good heavens, no!" said Mirror-Belle. "It's the size of the palace swimming pool. Surely you could find me something more suitable." She looked around and then pointed out of the window. "That coconut shell would be just the job. I can't think why it's hanging from a tree."

"I can't get you that," said Ellen. "It's got fat and raisins and things in it, for the birds."

A suspicious look crossed Mirror-Belle's face at the mention of birds. "For the golden goose, perhaps?" she said.

Ellen decided to change the subject back to Mirror-Belle's bath. "I've got a different idea," she said, and left the room.

She tiptoed past the sitting room, where

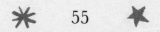

Granny and Grandpa were watching television, and into the kitchen. In a cupboard she found a pretty china sugar bowl with a pattern of bluebells on it. It wasn't the one Granny used every day, and Ellen hoped she wouldn't miss it.

Mirror-Belle was delighted with her flowery china bath. "It's almost as good as the one in the palace, which has roses and lilies on it," she said. She splashed around happily, and allowed herself to be dried with Ellen's face flannel. Then, "What about my nightdress?" she asked.

"I suppose you'll just have to get back

into your clothes," said Ellen, but Mirror-Belle would hear of no such thing. "Can't you make one for me out of rose petals?" she said.

"No," said Ellen. "It's not the time of year for roses, and I'm no good at sewing. Granny is, though," she added, suddenly remembering the clothes-peg dolls she used to play with when she was little, and the dresses Granny made for them.

The dolls used to be kept in an old wooden toy box under the spare-room bed. Ellen knelt down and looked. Yes! The box was still there; she recognized its brass handles. She pulled it out and rummaged inside, while Mirror-Belle shivered and said, "Do hurry up! I'm freezing!"

At the bottom of the box Ellen found the five clothes-peg dolls. She took them out and lifted Mirror-Belle down to the floor to show them to her. Four of the dolls had quite plain cotton dresses, but the fifth had a shiny purple one; Ellen remembered Granny making it from a silk tie that Grandpa didn't like.

Mirror-Belle's eyes lit up and she practically ripped the purple dress off the doll, then pulled it over her own head.

"Now, all that remains to be found is the royal bed," she said. "And I think I've spotted it." She ran under the big bed and climbed into one of Ellen's slippers. "I don't expect the giants will look for me here," she said.

"Would you like one of my socks as a sleeping bag?" asked Ellen, who was beginning to enjoy herself. It was a bit like having the very latest walkie-talkie doll to play with, even though Mirror-Belle was rather a bossy doll. Ellen actually felt disappointed when Granny called her away for a game of cards.

"Don't forget my cocoa!" Mirror-Belle called out after her, but when Ellen came back to the bedroom she was fast asleep.

The following morning Mirror-Belle announced that she was going to search high and low for the golden goose. "It's a good thing I've got you to help me, Ellen," she said. "You can look in all the high-up places."

But Ellen had other plans for the day: Granny and Grandpa had promised to take her out to the local safari park.

Mirror-Belle looked sulky when she heard this, but then her face brightened. "I suppose it's quite cunning of you to get the giants out of the way, so that I can carry out my search in peace," she said.

Ellen began to worry. "You're not to mess up the house," she warned Mirror-Belle. "And what will you eat and drink all day?"

"You'll have to see to that," said Mirror-Belle. "Whoever heard of a princess getting her own meals?"

Ellen managed to scrounge a few bits of food before she set out with Granny and Grandpa: some Choc-o-Hoops from her own breakfast, a scraping of cheese from the sandwiches Granny was making for their picnic and a couple of grapes from the fruit bowl. She delivered them to Mirror-Belle on a tray that was really the lid

of a jam jar, and filled the cap of her shampoo bottle with water.

"I'd prefer cowslip cordial," said Mirror-Belle.

"Tough," said Ellen, surprising herself by answering back for once. Maybe it was easier than usual because Mirror-Belle was so much smaller than her. Feeling a bit guilty, she said, "I'll try and save you some goodies from the picnic."

Ellen enjoyed the safari park, but she couldn't help worrying what Mirror-Belle might be getting up to. She wished now that she had been hard-hearted enough to close her bedroom door before setting out.

"I'll put the kettle on," said Granny when they got back.

Ellen ran up to her bedroom, feeling relieved that the hall and stairs at least looked the same as when they had left.

"Mirror-Belle!" Ellen called out softly, going into the room and closing the door behind her.

"Nineteen, twenty, twenty-one," came Mirror-Belle's voice.

"I've got you some crisps and some Smarties," said Ellen.

"Be quiet a minute, I'm trying to count." The voice was coming from under the bed.

"Twenty-two, twenty-three, twenty-four. The greedy things! This is probably some poor human's life savings."

Ellen lay on her tummy and saw not just Mirror-Belle but a heap of chocolate coins – the kind that are covered in gold paper. An empty little gold net and a pair of gold nail scissors lay beside them.

"Where did you find those?" she asked.

"Wait till you see what else I've found," said Mirror-Belle, and she ran behind the toy box.

"Not the golden goose, I bet," said Ellen.

"No, but look at this golden hen!" said Mirror-Belle, coming back into view with a little round fluffy Easter chick in her arms.  "Unfortunately it seems to be dead," she said as she set it down beside the coins.

"It's not dead, it's just a toy," said Ellen. "I expect Granny and Grandpa were planning to give it to me for Easter – and the coins too. I'll have to put them back wherever you found them. It's a shame you cut the bag open."

Mirror-Belle wasn't listening. She had picked up the golden net and taken it back behind the toy box. A moment later she reappeared, dragging it after her. "Look at all this stolen treasure!" she said. Grunting with the effort, she emptied the net.

Ellen gasped in horror as out fell two pairs of gold cufflinks, a watch and a diamond ring.

"I'm sure I recognize this crown," said Mirror-Belle, putting the ring on her head with the diamond at the front. "I seem to remember it went missing from the palace a few years ago. And this clock looks familiar too."

"It's not a clock – it's Granny's best watch. And that's her ring, and Grandpa's cufflinks. Oh, Mirror-Belle, this is terrible! Where did you find them all?"

"I'm not telling you. You'll only go and put them back," said Mirror-Belle.

"Yes, of course I will. Straight away, before Granny and Grandpa miss them.

Go on, Mirror-Belle – you *must* tell me."

"Oh, very well," said Mirror-Belle, who was obviously finding it difficult to resist boasting about her skill as an explorer. "The coins and the golden hen were easy enough to find – they were in a bag under the giants' bed. But the treasure and the golden shears were another matter."

"What golden shears? Oh, you mean the scissors. Where were they?"

"I was just about to tell you. It's a good thing the beanstalk had given me so much climbing practice – though I must say, the white snake was even more difficult."

"What white snake? What are you talking about, Mirror-Belle? Do explain properly!"

"It wasn't actually a snake, I suppose – more of a long, slippery white rope, leading to the giants' treasure chest."

"I think you must mean a light flex," said Ellen. "Right, I'm off."

She scooped up everything that Mirror-Belle had collected.

"Stop! Whose side are you on?" Mirror-Belle protested, but Ellen ignored her.

Making sure to close the door behind

her this time, she crept along the landing and into her grandparents' bedroom. She could hear Granny calling her to tea, but she had to put the things back first.

Sure enough, there was a carrier bag under the bed. Inside it were a couple of boxes which must contain Easter eggs. Ellen slipped the fluffy chick and the bag of coins in beside them.

The "white snake" was, as she had suspected, the flex of Granny's bedside lamp. Beside the lamp was a round embroidered jewel box with an unzipped lid. Ellen put the ring, watch and cufflinks inside. She wasn't sure exactly where the scissors belonged but she put them down beside the box and hoped for the best.

Just then she heard footsteps on the stairs.

"Ellen! Where are you? Your tea's getting cold."

Ellen's heart was thumping. If Granny found her here, how would she explain what she was doing? She stood frozen, wondering whether to hide. Then she heard Granny tap at the door of the spare bedroom and go in.

Quickly and quietly, Ellen went downstairs and into the kitchen, where Grandpa was having his tea.

"Your gran's looking for you," he said, and a moment later Granny came in.

"That's funny . . . Oh, there you are, Ellen. Where have you been?"

Ellen muttered something about the bathroom. Granny didn't look too pleased, and Ellen noticed that she was holding the sugar basin in one hand. In her other hand was the jam-jar lid, containing some grape pips and a little bit of cheese.

"What's all this?" said Granny. "Am I not feeding you enough?"

Ellen felt herself go red, but Grandpa said, "Don't scold the lass. I bet she was having a dolls' tea party, weren't you, Ellen?"

Ellen agreed, even though she was too old for that sort of thing. She didn't like lying to her kind grandparents, but it seemed the best way out of a tricky situation.

Granny had made a delicious fruitcake, but Ellen decided against smuggling any of it out to Mirror-Belle. Instead, she would try to persuade her mirror friend to go home.

"You'll have to, Mirror-Belle," she told her after tea. "I can't get you any more food, and Granny's taken your bath back, and . . . well, you must realize that you're not going to find the golden goose."

But Mirror-Belle refused to give up. "Tomorrow I search the garden," she said. "Now, what flavour were those crisps you were telling me about, Ellen? I hope they're smoky dragon ones."

The next day was Easter Sunday. There was a big Easter egg for Ellen on the breakfast table, along with the fluffy chick and the bag of chocolate money.

"I'm sorry the bag broke open," said Granny. "It looked all right in the shop."

"Stop fussing. The lass doesn't mind," said Grandpa. He turned to Ellen and handed her a piece of paper. "Look what the Easter rabbit left in the garden," he said.

When she was little Ellen had believed in the Easter rabbit, but now she knew that it was Granny and Grandpa who hid the little eggs in the garden every year, with clues to help find them. The piece of paper would be the first clue. She unfolded it and read, in Grandpa's handwriting:

Red-y? On your marks, get set!
Come and get your feathers wet!

She was rather surprised that Grandpa couldn't spell the word "ready" – he had left out the "a" – but was too polite to mention it.

"You'd better start looking if you want

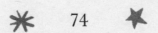 74

to beat those magpies to it," said Granny. "You know how they love anything shiny."

Ellen was about to run outside when she remembered Mirror-Belle. This could be a good opportunity for her to search the garden and discover that there was no golden goose hidden there after all.

"I'll just put on a cardigan," she said, and went up to her bedroom.

Mirror-Belle was still in her purple silk nightdress, lying in the slipper bed.

"You're interrupting my beauty sleep," she complained when Ellen picked her up. But as soon as she heard the plan she stopped fussing. "I'll need my binoculars," she said, so Ellen gave them to her and she snuggled down into the pocket of Ellen's thick, knitted cardigan.

Once they were outside, Mirror-Belle peeped out over the top of the pocket. "Where are you going?" she asked Ellen.

"To the bird bath," said Ellen. "This first clue's easy."

Sure enough, on the rim round the bird bath she found seven little eggs. They were all wrapped in red shiny paper, which explained Grandpa's funny spelling of the word "ready".

There was a piece of paper beside the eggs, and on it Ellen read the next clue:

Seven others, bright and blue,
In a nutshell wait for you.

"That's easy too!" she said, and went straight to the half-coconut which Mirror-Belle had wanted as her bath. Inside it were seven blue eggs.

"Excuse me," said Mirror-Belle, "but why are we hunting for eggs? I thought we were supposed to be finding the goose." Then she looked thoughtful. "Of course, it would be a different matter if we found some *golden* eggs. Then I could take one home and hatch it into a golden goose."

"It looks as though the next lot are green," said Ellen, and she read out the clue she had found in the coconut shell:

Small green eggs tell small old man,
"Try and catch us if you can."

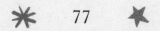

Ellen was puzzled at first, and Mirror-Belle said, "That's ridiculous. Eggs can't talk and, anyway, there aren't any small men in giant land."

"I've got it!" Ellen cried. "It must mean one of Grandpa's garden gnomes." One gnome had a wheelbarrow and another was smoking a pipe. Ellen searched around them but couldn't find any eggs. Then, "How stupid of me!" she said, and ran towards the fish pond.

"Slow down! I'm getting pocket-sick!" protested Mirror-Belle.

Standing beside the pond stood a garden gnome with a fishing rod, and at his feet were seven green eggs.

"That's why the clue says, 'Catch us if you can,'" explained Ellen. "Do you want to hear the next one?"

"If you insist," said Mirror-Belle with a yawn.

So Ellen read it out:

> *In the glass you may behold*
> *Seven eggs of shiny gold.*

Mirror-Belle stopped yawning. "The golden eggs!" she cried, and tried to climb out of Ellen's pocket.

"I wonder what 'the glass' means," said Ellen. "I think it could be a pane of the greenhouse."

"Nonsense!" said Mirror-Belle. "It's clearly referring to a mirror."

"But there aren't any mirrors in the garden," objected Ellen.

"I wouldn't be so sure," said Mirror-Belle, who was much more interested in the egg-hunt now that the next lot of eggs promised to be golden ones. "If you'd only put me down I'm sure that I'd find them in no time."

"All right," said Ellen, "but do be careful." She put Mirror-Belle down at the gnome's feet and said, "I'll see you back here in five minutes." Then she headed for the greenhouse, while Mirror-Belle ran off in the opposite direction.

There weren't any eggs inside the greenhouse. Ellen had just started looking around the outside of it when she heard a triumphant cry: "I've found them!"

Mirror-Belle was standing at the far end of the garden, holding a golden egg above her head. Ellen was surprised at how far she had travelled.

"I'm coming!" she called, and

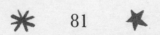

then she saw something else.
A magpie was flying down
from a tree just above
Mirror-Belle. It must
have spotted her and
decided she could be
good to eat.

"Watch out!" Ellen yelled, and started
to run. She saw the magpie land and then
take off again. Was Mirror-Belle in its
beak? She couldn't see.

Ellen reached the spot where she had
seen Mirror-Belle. There on the ground
was a cluster of golden eggs. She didn't
count them, but instead looked round for
Mirror-Belle.

"Well? What did you think of the clues?"
said Granny. She crossed the lawn and

took the piece of paper from Ellen's hand. "That's quite a good one," she said. "Did you spot Grandpa's secret mirror?"

"No," said Ellen. "Where is it?"

Granny pointed at a plant covered in pink flowers. It was a moment before Ellen saw the curved mirror which was standing behind it.

"Another of Grandpa's brainwaves," said Granny. "He was always disappointed that that peony didn't have more flowers, but this way it looks as if it's got twice the amount."

Ellen smiled – not at Grandpa's trick, but because she realized that Mirror-Belle must have disappeared safely into the mirror and not been caught by the magpie after all.

"Did you find all the eggs, then?" asked Granny.

"I think so," said Ellen, and displayed them proudly.

Granny counted them. "There's one missing," she said. "There should be seven of each colour, but you've only found six gold ones." She looked all around the peony and then gave up. "It must be those magpies!" she said.

"Yes, of course," said Ellen, but she knew that even if they found and searched the magpies' nest the missing golden egg would not be in it. Princess Mirror-Belle must have taken it back to mirror land with her. It was only a chocolate egg really, but Ellen couldn't help hoping that it would hatch into a golden goose.

About the Author and Illustrator

Julia Donaldson is one of the UK's most popular children's writers. Her award-winning books include *What the Ladybird Heard, The Snail and the Whale* and *The Gruffalo*. She has also written many children's plays and songs, and her sell-out shows based on her books and songs are a huge success. She was the Children's Laureate from 2011 to 2013, campaigning for libraries and for deaf children, and creating a website for teachers called picturebookplays.co.uk. Julia and her husband Malcolm divide their time between Sussex and Edinburgh. You can find out more about Julia at www.juliadonaldson.co.uk.

Lydia Monks studied Illustration at Kingston University, graduating in 1994 with a first-class degree. She is a former winner of the Smarties Bronze Award for *I Wish I Were a Dog* and has illustrated many books by Julia Donaldson. Her illustrations have been widely admired.

Also available

For younger readers

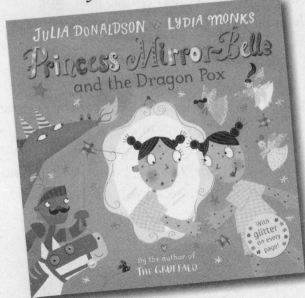